Little Learners

My First Animal Tales

stories to read

words to learn

Colour
Library
Direct

This edition published in 1999 by Colour Library Direct
Produced by Quadrillion Publishing Ltd,
Godalming Business Centre, Woolsack Way,
Godalming, Surrey GU7 1XW.

Design: Fiona Land
Editorial and new text: Debbie Fox
Illustrations: *The Dolphin Daytrip, Nobody Wants to Play*
and *Treasure Hunt* by Colleen Payne; *Thirsty Work* by Mary Lonsdale;
Little Kittens in the Dark and *Little Kittens and the Big Cats*
by Teri Gower; *Bunnies in the Snow* by Johnathan Satchell.
Original text: *The Dolphin Daytrip* by Colleen Payne; *Thirsty Work,
Nobody Wants to Play* and *Treasure Hunt* by Jenny Millington; *Little
Kittens in the Dark* and *Little Kittens and the Big Cats* by Kate Brookes;
Bunnies in the Snow by Emma Satchell.

Ref. No. 8580

ISBN 1-84100-154-6

Printed in Hong Kong

CONTENTS

The Dolphin Day Trip

Something bright and shiny was glistening on the sea bed.

"I wonder what that is?" thought Kipper and he dived down to have a look. It was a golden key.

"You've found it!" cried a little voice behind him.

The little mermaid had been looking everywhere for the lost key.

"Hello," she said. "My name is Coral. You have found the key to King Neptune's garden. You must come to the palace with me because the King will want to thank you."

King Neptune was waiting to meet
the clever dolphin who had found
the key.

"You must stay with us all day," he
said. "I will show you my garden
palace."

Kipper was very excited.

"And I will grant a wish as your
reward," laughed the King.

Kipper had never seen such a
beautiful garden before.

"I wish my dolphin friends
could see this!" he said.

"If that is your wish, then so
they shall!" cried the King.

"Coral will swim to them and
bring them back here."

Not long afterwards Sonar, Seaweed and Bottlenose were playing with Kipper in the palace garden. The little mermaids swam and dived with the dolphins. It was such a magical day.

"Thank you for granting my wish," smiled Kipper.

"And thank you for a wonderful day trip," called the dolphin friends.

what can you find?

fish

mermaid

castle

crown

dolphin

words to learn

bright	garden
shiny	lost
sea bed	clever
dive	wish
key	friends
behind	swim

Thirsty Work

The sun was shining brightly on a hot summer's day.

"I'm thirsty," said Drummer to his friends. "Let's go down to the stream and have a drink of water."

When the ponies got to the stream,
they found that all the
water had disappeared!

"What's happened?" said Drummer.
The frogs didn't know. They were
just as unhappy as the ponies.

The ponies searched along the bank
of the stream. They found a huge pile
of mud and twigs. No wonder the
stream was dry!

"We need Ralph's help," said Duchess.

"I'm here," said Ralph. "What seems to be the trouble?"

"Our stream is blocked," Duchess explained. "And we're so thirsty! Do you think you could clear it for us?"

"Oh yes," barked Ralph. "I can dig out all that mud in no time."

Ralph jumped slap bang into the middle of the mud!

His paws were working fast, flinging the mud on the bank. He was really enjoying himself!

He called out to Dora, "Can you help me? Could you carry all these twigs away in your beak?"

Dora was only too pleased to help.

Soon the stream was flowing again. The thirsty ponies could have a drink at last.

"Thank you Ralph and Dora," said Cassie with a huge sigh of relief.

Ralph and Dora were feeling hot after all their hard work. Splash! They both jumped into the water to cool off. To Ralph splashing about was as much fun as digging up mud!

what can you find?

frog

flower

pony

leaf

dog

words to learn

hot	mud
summer	dry
stream	dig
drink	middle
water	paws
frog	beak
unhappy	work

31

Little Kittens in the Dark

"Veda, Oscar, Rufus, Lullaby!"
Mother Cat was worried about her
little kittens. They didn't usually

stay in the woods so late. She called again. Where could they be?

Sally Squirrel was also worried about her friends, "I'll go and find them," she said.

The little kittens were so busy
exploring the woods that they
didn't notice the sun going down.
It was only when they heard the old
owl hoot and saw a badger coming
out of its set that they realised it
was night-time.

"We want to go home," miaowed Rufus, Lullaby and Oscar.

Veda looked around. She didn't know which path would take them home.

"I think we are lost," she sighed.

The frightened kittens followed a winding path that led to a wheat field. The wheat was so tall that even when the kittens stood on each other's shoulders they couldn't see over the top of it!

Suddenly there was a loud rustle. Hares and field mice scurried to their nests. The kittens could see quite well in the dark, but they were too scared to look!

"Found you at last," said Sally Squirrel when she saw the kittens huddled together.

"How did you find us?" asked Veda.

"Old Owl and Badger showed me which path you took," answered Sally.

"Can you take us home now?" the kittens miaowed.

The little kittens followed Sally through the woods. Old Owl hooted to tell all the animals that the kittens were safe. In the distance the kittens could see their home and their mother sitting on the wall.

Mother Cat gave them all a very big hug and Oscar asked, "May we explore the woods again tomorrow?"

Can you guess what the other kittens said?

what can you find?

cat

badger

owl

wheat

hare

words to learn

kittens

late

busy

sun

owl

home

path

tall

loud

mice

dark

mother

wall

Little Kittens and the Big Cats

Veda, Rufus, Oscar and Lullaby
scampered along the path that led
to the road. Mother Cat watched as
they stopped at the side of the road,
looked left and right, and then
looked left again.

When it was safe, they crossed the road to the zoo. The little kittens were excited. They were going to see the big cats.

"Look, there's a lion," said Veda. "I wish I had a mane of hair like that." Veda tried to fluff up the grey fur round her face with her paws.

"I wish I was as big as a lion," said Rufus as he balanced on the lion's huge paw.

Lion

Oscar and Lullaby found the tiger. She was eating her lunch. It was feeding time at the zoo.

After she had finished chewing her meat, the tiger let out a huge growl. "I wish I could growl like that," said

Tiger

Oscar. He took a deep breath, opened his mouth wide, but instead of growling, he just miaowed! Lullaby thought this was very funny and couldn't stop laughing.

At first the
kittens didn't
see the spotted leopard
lying on a branch high in
a tree. He was swinging
his long, long tail
backwards and
forwards.

"I wish my tail was longer," said Lullaby, and she ran round and round in circles trying to catch her tail. This made her very dizzy.

Leopard

"Where's Oscar?" asked Lullaby as they headed for home. Somewhere above their heads they heard a faint growl. The three kittens looked up. There, stretched out on a branch, was Oscar. His tail was swinging backwards and forwards, backwards and forwards.

"Come down," they shouted. It was feeding time at home!

what can you find?

bird

signpost

lion

kitten

words to learn

road	face
left	tiger
right	lunch
zoo	meat
cats	mouth
hair	tree
fur	tail

Nobody Wants to Play

Zack was bored playing on his own. He looked for Biscuit. He wanted him to join in the game. "Not now," said Biscuit, "I'm eating my breakfast."

Bella and Tansy were dozing in
their basket. Zack woke them up.
"Come outside and play!" he barked.

"Not now," said Bella closing her eyes again, "we're much too tired. You'd better come back later."

Zack found Freda in her pond
in the garden.

"Will you come and play with me?"
he asked. But Freda said she was
just too busy looking for flies.

Sidney looked down from the
branch of a tree.

"Before you ask," he said to Zack,
"I'm busy counting nuts, so I can't
come and play either."

Zack laid down on the lawn and put his head on his paws. He was feeling very sad and lonely.

"Why won't anyone play with me?" he thought. "Don't they like me anymore?"

Suddenly Bella and Biscuit ran up, with Tansy not far behind them. Sidney scampered down from his tree and Freda hopped out of the pond.

"We were only joking!" they all said. "Of course we want to play with you!"

Zack didn't mind when they all started to chase him round and round the garden. They were all having fun!

what can you find?

dogs' basket

bin

pie

ball

toad

words to learn

game   pond

breakfast   branch

play   nuts

eyes   sad

tired   chase

Treasure Hunt

"I need your help," said Sidney to Bella. "Last winter I buried some nuts in the garden, but I can't remember where."

Bella was happy to help. She dug a few small holes where the cabbages were growing, but she couldn't find any hidden nuts.

She dug a bigger hole in the onion patch. But there was still no sign of Sidney's nut store. Where could it be?

Zack joined in the hunt. He scratched around in the flower bed, leaving trampled and broken flowers behind him.

Meanwhile, Tansy decided to try the lawn. Making a hole in the grass was hard work and Tansy had to dig in several places.

Along came Biscuit. When he saw
what the other puppies had done to
the garden, he was very annoyed.
"Look at the mess you've made!"
he said angrily, "You will have to
clear it up."

The puppies did their best to tidy up before anyone saw what they had done. Zack even tried to mend some of the broken flowers.

"Oh no," wailed Sidney, "I've just remembered. I buried those nuts in the woods, not in the garden!"

And he ran off to find them for himself.

what can you find?

cabbage

blackbird

bush

squirrel

onions

words to learn

help

winter

happy

small

hole

flower

grass

mess

tidy

broken

Bunnies in the Snow

"Brrr, I'm freezing," said Violet, shivering. The little bunnies were on their way home.

"It is very cold," said William. "Wait

a minute, what's this on my nose?"
"I think it's called a snowflake,"
answered Violet. Suddenly lots of
snow began to fall.

The bunnies were amazed when the snow formed a white blanket over the ground.

"Let's have some fun!" said Basil, as he began to roll and play.

"Look at this!" cried Violet as
she kicked up a spray of snow
which covered William from his
ears to his tail.

"A snow bunny," giggled Heather.
William gave Violet an angry look.

The snow was falling fast.

"Will it last forever?" sighed Heather.

"I hope not, or we will never find our

way home," grumbled William. The

little bunnies were alarmed when they

saw that their path home had

disappeared!

"What's that noise?" cried Basil.

The bunnies looked at the snowy sky and saw their friends Marianne and Michael coming in to land.

With the help of the geese, the
little bunnies reached the edge of
the garden. But when they lifted
their little noses, they saw a large
stranger looming over them.

"Who's that in our garden?"
squeaked Violet.

"Don't worry," laughed Michael.
"I've met his type before. He's
called a snowman and he's not at
all scary."

As the bunnies hopped towards their hutch, they noticed strange footprints leading to the open door. "Who's in our hutch?" shouted William.

"Good afternoon," replied a muffled voice.

There was a rustle and a snuffle, and from under the pile of straw appeared the face of their old friend Morris Mole!

"Just keeping the hutch warm for you," he explained.

So the little bunnies snuggled down too and were soon feeling cosy and warm.

what can you find?

fence

snowman

goose

rabbit

words to learn

cold	ears
minute	angry
nose	sky
snow	geese
white	door
ground	warm

91